CLARA BUTTON

AND THE

WEDDING DAY SURPRISE

written by AMY DE LA HAYE

illustrated by EMILY SUTTON

V&A Publishing

It was the school holidays, and Clara Button was busy doing what she liked to do best. She was making clothes and hats for her toy animals. It was not easy to design a coat that would fit a giraffe!

Her older brother Ollie was also doing what he liked best – inventing! Scattered around him were pieces of old clocks, tubes, springs and even old taps.

While they were upstairs, the postman walked up the garden path with some letters.

Later that morning Mum said, 'We've all been invited
to a *very* special wedding. There will be a procession
and a feast and dancing.'

'What shall I wear?' Clara asked her Mum excitedly.

'You can choose one of your best dresses. Ollie, you will have
to wear your school trousers as they are your smartest ones.'

Ollie grumbled to himself and continued working on his invention.

Clara was not sure she would ever get married, but it was fun to imagine all sorts of dreamy wedding gowns.

Clara went upstairs to plan her outfit.
She tried on the most unusual combinations,
but nothing seemed quite right. Eventually,
she chose a blue dress decorated with little
purple flowers around the neck.

The next day was Saturday and Mum took Clara and Ollie to a market.

Clara wanted to find something special to wear with her dress to the wedding. She asked Mum if they could go into the haberdashery.

Meanwhile, Ollie had found a stall that looked fascinating.
'Wow! Where did you get all this brilliant stuff from?' he asked.
'I've collected these fine specimens from countries across the
world,' the man behind the stall said proudly.

Later, Clara asked Ollie what he had bought.
'I can't show you... it's top secret,' he announced,
as he clutched his bag close to his body.

The evening before the wedding Clara was putting the finishing touches to her outfit. She decorated her shoes with the sparkly jewels and sequins she'd bought at the haberdashery. They looked splendid but what else could she do?

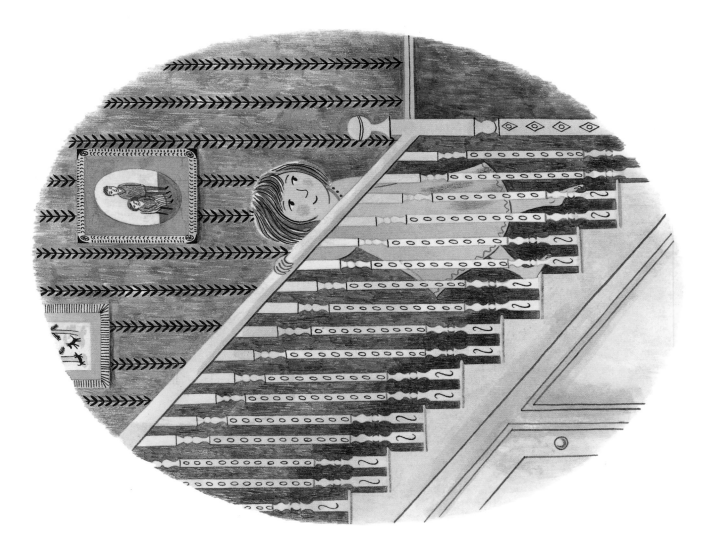

Perhaps she could make her hair more colourful? In fact, the purple food dye Mum had used to ice the cakes would match with her dress perfectly. She tiptoed down the stairs to the kitchen.

Very carefully Clara rubbed the dye into her hair. 'Oh no!' she exclaimed as she looked down and saw big purple stains on her dress... Her hands were stained purple too.

That night Clara had a horrid dream. She was in the church at the wedding but she didn't feel quite right.

When Clara woke up, she had a brainwave. She turned the stains on her dress into flower patterns using her felt-tip pens. Feeling a little nervous she went downstairs.

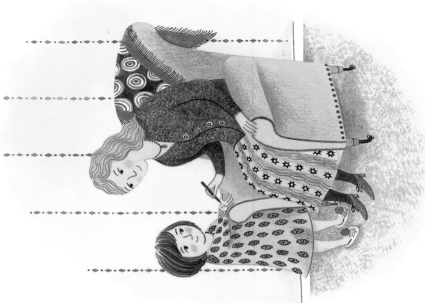

'What a pretty dress,' said Mum. Then she looked a bit closer.

'I got dye on it,' said Clara. 'But then I made the splodges into flowers.'

Mum began to get cross but then she smiled. As usual Clara had turned a disaster into something fantastic.

Taking Clara's hands
she transformed the purple marks
into beautiful patterns.

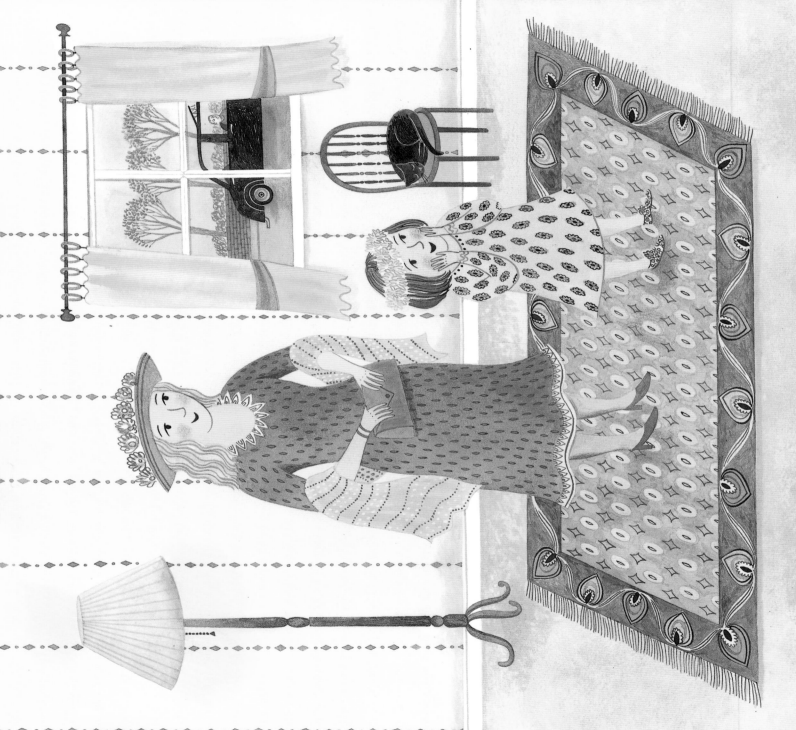

Finally Mum and Clara were ready to leave. Ollie appeared and they both gasped... His school trousers might be rather boring, but the musical, confetti-throwing, drum-banging machine he had invented certainly was not!

They arrived at the wedding in a taxi.

The groom was on horseback: he was wearing

magnificent clothes and jewels – and so was the horse.

The wedding was very different from how Clara had imagined it.

It was a Hindu wedding, and it was wonderfully colourful.

Clara grinned – she looked just right at this wedding!
Everyone loved Ollie's invention and he and Clara joined
in the wedding procession.

And, to Clara's astonishment,
the bride's hands were painted like hers!

CLARA BUTTON

and the

WEDDING DAY SURPRISE

written by AMY DE LA HAYE

illustrated by EMILY SUTTON